200141

AR Quiz

IL **LG**

BL **5.3**

Pts. **0.5**

PERSONAL COMPUTERS

REVISED EDITION

A TRUE **BOOK**

by

**Charnan and
Tom Kazunas**

Children's Press®

A Division of Grolier Publishing

New York London Hong Kong Sydney
Danbury, Connecticut

Reading Consultant
Linda Cornwell
Learning Resource Consultant
Indiana Department of
Education

For Helen Foster James

One of the many tiny
parts from a computer

Library of Congress Cataloging-in-Publication Data

Kazunas, Tom.
    Personal Computers / by Tom and Charnan Kazunas. — Rev. ed.
    p. cm. — (True book)
    Includes bibliographical references and index.
    ISBN 0-516-21938-3 (lib. bdg.)   0-516-26859-7 (pbk.)
    1. Microcomputers—Juvenile literature. [1. Microcomputers.
2. Computers.] I. Kazunas, Charnan II. Title. III. Series.
    QA76.23.K39 2000
    004.16—dc21   00-060383

Contents

In the 1940s, ENIAC filled a large room.

Computers Then and Now

Here's a riddle for you: What used to fill a whole room, today fits on your lap, and tomorrow might be smaller than a pencil eraser?

If you said a computer, you were right! One of the earliest computers, called ENIAC (Electronic Numerical

Integrator and Computer), was built in 1945. It weighed as much as six elephants and filled a room 50 feet long by 30 feet wide. Today's computers fit easily on your lap. And the U.S. Army is working on a computer of the future that will be no bigger than a vitamin pill!

Even as computers are getting smaller, they are getting better. A small laptop computer is faster and more powerful than the enormous ENIAC was fifty years ago.

Today, a laptop computer is much smaller and faster than the first computers.

Countless

In the 1940s, scientists believed that *just a dozen computers* would be enough to serve all the people in the world. Today, there are *more than 556 million computers* being used in homes, schools, and offices around the globe.

Computers

And this doesn't include all the larger computers in the world. Nor does it include the microprocessors used in our VCRs, washing machines, cars, trains, and airplanes. Computers are everywhere!

Computers, Big and Little

One hundred years ago, people did almost all of their writing and number calculating by hand. Today, computers do much of this for us.

Some computers are very large. Supercomputers, mainframe computers, and

An abacus is a quick way to
do calculations by hand.

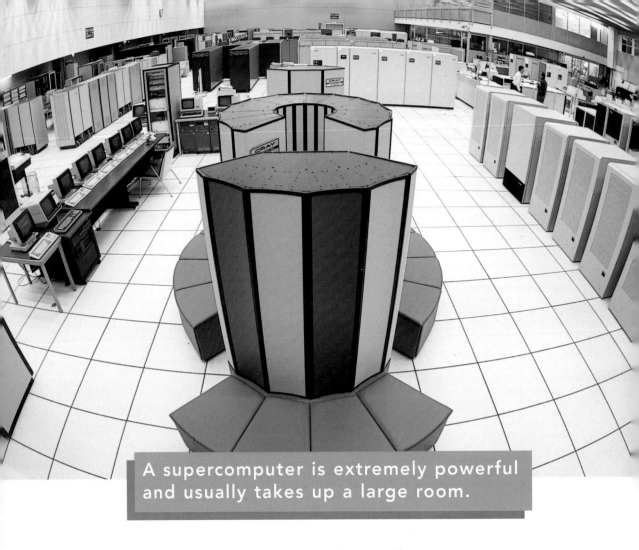

A supercomputer is extremely powerful and usually takes up a large room.

minicomputers handle com-plicated tasks or allow many people to work together at the same time.

Personal computers (called "PCs" for short) are much smaller. They are designed to let just one person work at a time. The computers that you use at school and at home are PCs. By using a PC, anyone can tap into a computer's tremendous power.

There are several different sizes of PCs. Those that fit on an ordinary desktop are called desktop computers. Laptop computers are small enough to

fit on your lap, while notebook
computers are about the size of
a book. Smaller still are pocket
or palm-sized computers, which
can slip easily into a pocket.

But whatever their size, all
personal computers are
made up of the same basic
components.

Examples of desktop (opposite), laptop (above), and notebook computers (right).

Computers in Space

The space program in the 1960s and 1970s helped bring about today's small personal computers. Spaceships could not take off,

MOD

travel in space, or land safely without the help of computers. Large computers work fine in the control centers on the ground. But only very small computers would fit inside a tiny space capsule or shuttle. So scientists found ways to build smaller computers for astronauts to use.

What's a Component?

Every PC is made up of several different parts, or components. These components are known as the computer hardware.

The central processing unit, or CPU, is the heart of the computer. It does the real work—multiplying, dividing, and such—faster than a human can. Connected to the CPU is

a permanently installed hard disk drive. The hard disk (or "hard drive") stores the programs and data, or information, that tell the computer how to do its work.

The keyboard is the part that looks like a typewriter. When you type commands of words, letters, and numbers, you are telling your computer what to do. Most computers also have a mouse, which is a small box connected to the computer by a wire. Moving the mouse or pressing the buttons on it are other ways to give your computer commands.

The monitor has a screen like a television. This screen

You can give a computer commands by typing on the keyboard (left) or clicking a mouse (right).

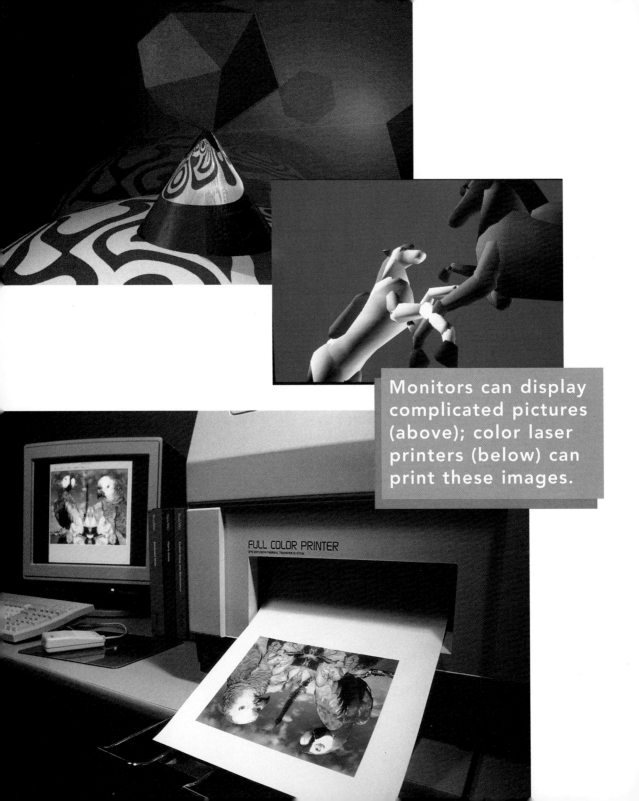

Monitors can display complicated pictures (above); color laser printers (below) can print these images.

displays the numbers, words, and pictures produced by the computer.

The printer is used to produce a printed hard copy of the computer's work. When you save a text on the computer, it is called "soft copy," but when you print it out, it's called "hard copy." When you use a PC to write a story or a letter, you can use the printer to make a copy for your teacher, a copy for your parents, or a copy for your best friend.

Peripherals

Computers use many other special gadgets, called peripherals. Modems connect computers to telephone lines so that computers can "talk" to each other. Scanners take pictures that your computer can use or display. Joysticks help you play computer games.

Electronic pens make it possible to draw on a desk pad or directly on the screen. You can even play or compose music with an *electronic piano keyboard* connected to your PC! Peripherals allow people to do more with their computers.

Introducing... Software!

The list of things you can do with a personal computer is almost endless. You can write a story and draw a picture. You can figure out math problems, keep track of all your cousins' addresses, fly an imaginary airplane, and play a game of checkers.

You can use PC programs to help you with homework.

Placing a floppy
disk in a computer.

But a computer can't do anything without a software program. A program is the list of instructions that tells a computer exactly how to do any given job. The general name for computer programs is software.

Some software programs still come on floppy disks that you can load into your computer. The PC either reads the floppy disk directly, or copies the program from the floppy

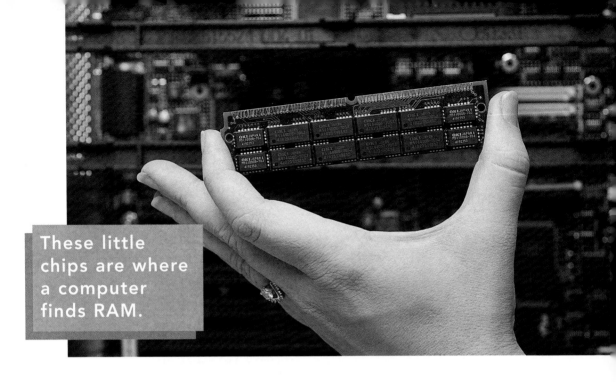

These little chips are where a computer finds RAM.

to the hard disk drive. While the computer uses a program, the computer stores it in RAM (random access memory). You can think of RAM as a chalkboard that the computer can write on, read from, and change anytime it wants.

Now, many software pro-grams are so big, they would not fit on a floppy disk. These programs are supplied on their own storage devices, called CD-ROMs. They store large amounts of information and can't be erased acciden-tally.

ROM stands for "read only memory." This is permanent memory, which can also be built into the chips inside a computer. This information

A CD-ROM can store an entire encyclopedia.

stays the same even when the computer is turned off, so the computer can remember what to do when it is turned back on again. You can think of ROM as a book from which the computer can read again and again.

One special kind of program is installed at the factory on the hard disk drive of every PC. This program is called the operating system. An operating system is like a magic wand that wakes up the computer. It says to the PC: "You are a computer! You have a keyboard! A monitor! A printer! Use your power!" Without an operating system, a computer can't run any other programs.

Software Everywhere

Word processing programs are one of the most popular kinds of software. They help you produce perfectly typed and spelled stories and letters. You can correct mistakes, move words, sentences, and paragraphs, and even check your spelling, all by pressing a few keys on the keyboard.

Computers are great
tools for writing.

Paint without a mess
on a computer.

Painting programs are terrific, too. Just by pressing the keys on your keyboard (or the buttons on your mouse), you can make pictures using computer pens, pencils, and paintbrushes. You can use many different colors. You can draw your own pictures, or use patterns that the computer provides. When you are done, you can print a hard copy of your artwork to hang on the refrigerator.

Math programs help you learn about numbers—adding, subtracting, multiplying, and dividing. At the same time, you can play exciting games! You might think you are just scoring points to win or lose, but you are also learning about how numbers work together.

Some software programs let you imagine that you are flying in a spaceship or traveling on a wagon train.

Computers are great for games, too.

You can play checkers or chess or card games on a PC. You can search for hidden treasure, play nine innings of baseball, or hurry through a maze, one step ahead of a hungry blob.

A Brave New Electronic World

By itself, a PC is a very powerful machine. When PCs communicate with other computers, they create a network that is even more powerful. Through a network, a single PC can share all the information that's available on any other network PC.

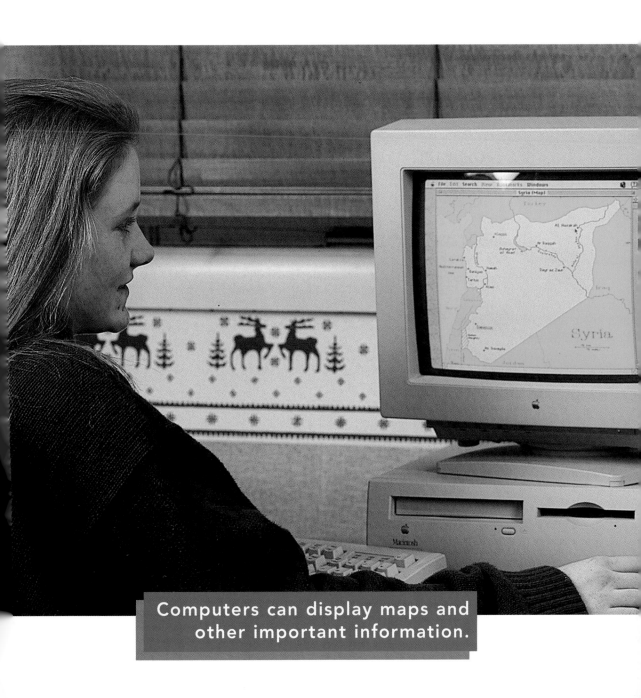

Computers can display maps and other important information.

For example, you can buy an electronic encyclopedia for your home PC. But through a network, you can access an entire library with your computer! And more—you can shop for summer camps or new clothes. You can order airplane tickets or check out the scores of soccer matches in Argentina. You can "talk" to people around the world.

The world of personal computers is an amazing place.

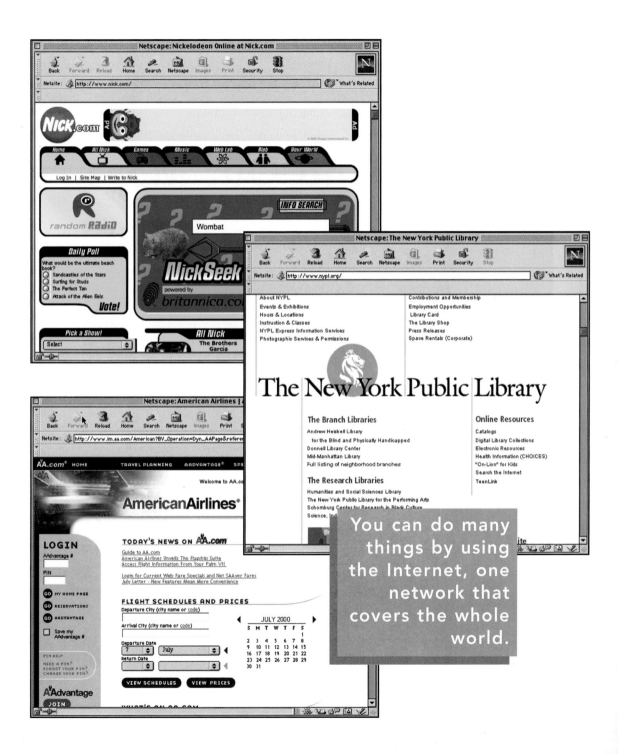

You can do many things by using the Internet, one network that covers the whole world.

To Find Out More

Here are some additional resources to help you learn more about personal computers:

 **Books**

 **Internet Sites**

Dummies Press Families. **PCs for Kids & Parents.** IDG Books Worldwide, 1997.

Negrino, Tom, and Wendy Sharp. **Macs for Kids and Parents.** IDG Books Worldwide, 1997.

Sabbeth, Carol. **Kids Computer Creations: Using Your Computer for Art & Craft Fun.** Williamson Publishing Company, 1995.

Berit's Best Sites for Children
http://www.beritsbest.com/

An index of fun and informative sites designed for children.

Children's Shareware and More
http://www.kidsdomain.com/

A collection of shareware—software made available over the Internet—and information about computer programs for children.

Do Spiders Live on the World Wide Web?
http://www.ipl.org/youth/ storyhour/spiders/cover. html

The Internet Public Library created this "book" showing the usual and the computer meaning of words such as "mouse" and "window."

The Internet Public Library Youth Division
http://www.ipl.org/youth/

Links to lots of information on just about any subject.

Kidscom
http://www.kidscom.com

A place where you can send messages to world leaders, play games, read and share your favorite jokes, and chat with other kids.

Yahooligans
http://www.yahooligans. com

This site maintained by the Yahoo web index contains dozens of links to computer-related subjects, and guides you to websites designed for children.

Important Words

component a part of a computer system, such as a monitor, keyboard, or printer

CPU the "brain" of a computer that does the actual computing — multiplying, dividing, etc.

data numbers or other information used by a computer

hardware a computer and all its physical parts

network a group of computers connected by telephone wires in order to share information

peripheral an added-on computer device, such as a scanner, modem, or joystick

software the general name for computer programs. A program is a list of instructions that tells a computer how to do a given job

Index

Meet the Authors

Charnan and Tom Kazunas are married and live in Madison, Wisconsin, with their daughters, Ariel and Hana, their dog Sam, and their two computers.

Tom's computer is new and fast and powerful. Tom uses it to solve complicated math problems, design books, visit websites, do research, and play all kinds of games.

Charnan's computer is old and slow and tired. Every morning when she turns it on, it says "Disk boot failure." This means Charnan has time to walk the dog, make a cup of tea, and write a postcard to a friend. By then her computer is warmed up, and Charnan can get to work writing books.